Mind the Gap

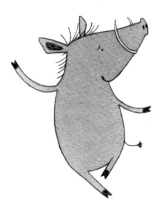

Poems by Roger McGough

Illustrations by Natalie Kilany

Contents

Sid	3
I'm Seven	4
Tonsillitis Days	5
Itch	6
Aunt-Eater	7
Tickle Your Granny	8
Sweet Teeth	9
Feeding the Ducks	10
Garden Pasta	12
Hogging Hedges	13
Pablo, the Wild Boar Who Wasn't	14
Goldfish	18
Rude Kangaroo	19
The Figment Tree	20
The Tooth Fairy	21
What Is It?	22
The Garbage Monster	24
Mind the Gap	25
Hide and Seek	26
Friends	27
The Friendship	28
Stop, Thief!	29
Posters on the platform	30

Sid

How did you know my name was Sid?
That's a fact I've always hid.

When asked my name I always say
"Tom" then look the other way.

For reasons that I'll now explain
I never liked Sid as a Christian name.

Sidney rhymes with "kidney"
So I keep it under my hat,

And "Sid, Sid, the dustbin lid"
I'm sick to death of that.

So how did you know my name was Sid
Something that I've always hid?

"Because that's what the poem's called."

I'm Seven

I'm seven, I'm seven
I'll never be six again

I used to be five
And I used to be four

I'll never be three
Or two any more

I used to be one
But those days are long gone

Next year I'll be eight
Then I'll be nine

And the year after that
I'll be ten

I'm seven, I'm seven
I'm in seventh heaven
And I'll never be six again.

Tonsillitis Days

Sometimes I think of my tonsils
And wonder where they are,
Left behind in the hospital
When I went home by car.

Do they still hang out together
Or did they go their separate ways?
I don't miss them, to be honest
Those tonsillitis days.

Itch

My sister had an itch
　I asked if it was catching.

"Catch," she said, and threw it
　Now I'm the one who's scratching.

Aunt-Eater

Aunt-eater, aunt-eater
Where have you been?
Aunt Liz took you walkies
And hasn't been seen.

Nor has Aunt Mary,
Aunt Lil or Aunt Di.
Aunt-eater, aunt-eater
Why the gleam in your eye?

Tickle Your Granny

Cut the cackle
and get the gist,

Heat the kettle
and wet the wrist,

Raise the hackle
and cock the snook,

Shake the rattle
and sling the hook,

Trim the tackle
and nook the cranny,

Lick the pickle
and tickle your granny.

Sweet Teeth

Grandma ate bowlfuls of toffees
From morning till night she'd not stop
Sprinkled with spoonfuls of sugar
And honey drizzled on top.

Grandad he preferred fruit gums
Drenched in tomato sauce
Or liquorice allsorts in mayonnaise
(Their teeth are in the cupboard, of course).

Feeding the Ducks

We're off to feed the ducks,
The ducks, the ducks.
We're off to feed the ducks,
Hear them quacking in the rain.

What shall we feed the ducks?
The ducks, the ducks?
What shall we feed the ducks?
Soggy bread means tummy pain.

Snails and slugs and insects,
Worms and hard-boiled eggs,
Turnip-tops and lettuce,
Acorns, seed and grain.

We've been to feed the ducks,
The ducks, the ducks.
We've been to feed the ducks,
And they quacked "Please come again."

Don't feed
bread to
the ducks.

Garden Pasta

Blackbirds adore spaghetti
They love to eat it raw
Tug worms out of the soil
Then sing, 'cos there's plenty more.

Hogging Hedges

Hedgehogs
tend to hog
the edges
of hedges.

Whereas a hole
near the verge is
where a mole
emerges.

Toads on roads
who ignore
the highway code
have been known
to explode.

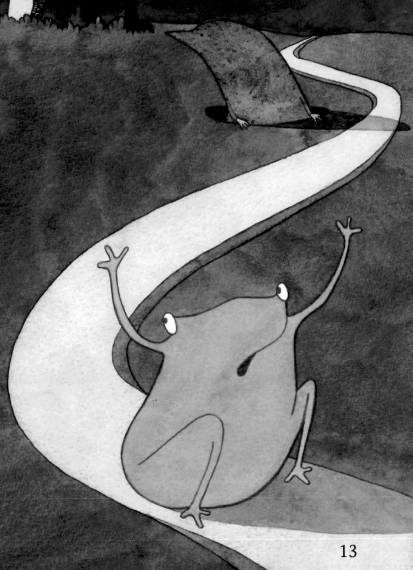

Pablo, the Wild Boar Who Wasn't

Pablo was a boar
but wild, not at all,
When faced with a mouse
He'd roll into a ball.

For he was a softie
from the day he was born,
Polite and well-mannered
he weathered the scorn

of those as fierce
as their name implied.
Wild? Why, he couldn't
be wild if he tried.

His tusks were gentle,
His eyes were bright,
When he danced a jig
His hooves were light.

But he could sniff mushrooms
and gather them fast,
And at snuffling for truffles
he was unsurpassed.

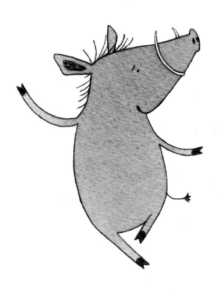

One day while out foraging
he was beguiled
by a pretty young gilt,
reassuringly wild.

His tusks were gentle,
His eyes were bright,
When they danced a jig
His hooves were light.

Now the sow goes out hunting
while he cares for the litter,
Pablo the mild,
wild boar baby-sitter.

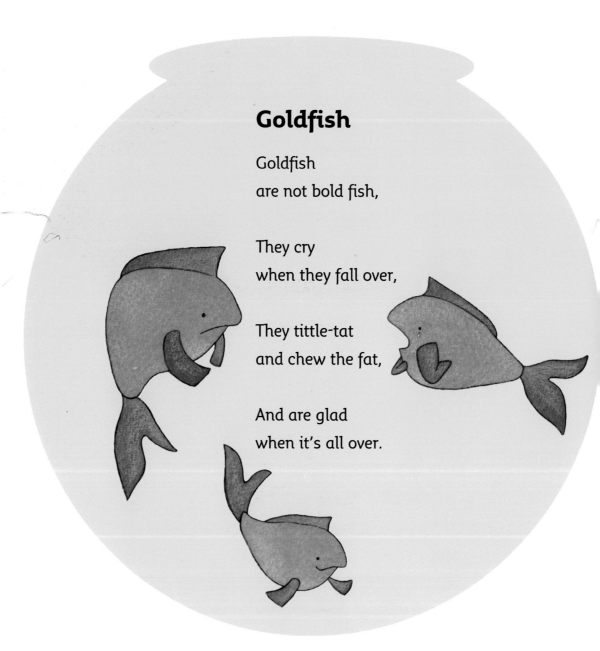

Goldfish

Goldfish
are not bold fish,

They cry
when they fall over,

They tittle-tat
and chew the fat,

And are glad
when it's all over.

18

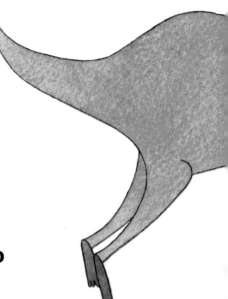

Rude Kangaroo

Kan ga roo

Kan ga roo

Kindly stop

jump ing

I'm talking

to you.

The Figment Tree

I believe in fairies
And each evening after tea,
At the bottom of the garden
Beneath the figment tree,
Alone, I sit and wonder
If they believe in me.

The Tooth Fairy

One day, the Tooth Fairy,
Not looking where she was flying,
Flew straight into a toadstool
And knocked out a front tooth.

That night, she put it under her pillow,
Made a wish and fell asleep.
On waking, she rubbed her eyes
And surprise, surprise!
It was still there.

What Is It?

I walked down the lane
and then I saw it,
Turned into a field
and there it was.

I climbed up the hill
and then I saw it,
Scrambled down the other side
and there it was.

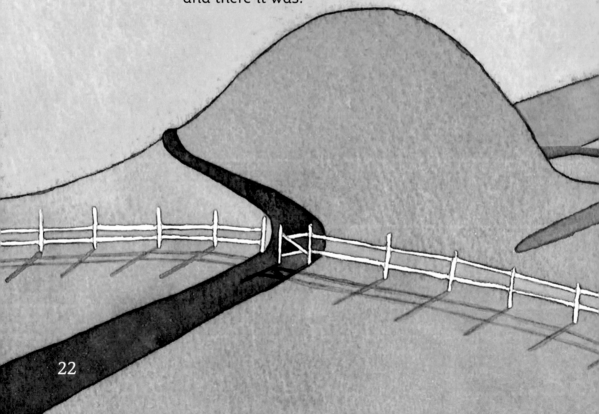

I dashed across the bridge
and then I saw it,
Reached the river bank
and there it was.

I ran towards the house
and then I saw it,
Hurried up the garden path
and there it was.

I collapsed into a chair
and then I saw it,
Closed my eyes, fell asleep
and there it was.

The Garbage Monster

To gobble up your waste
is my ambition. You need me.

A monster on a mission
I love the taste. Please feed me.

Armed with metal teeth
I grind it into paste.

Nothing goes to waste
when garbage is faced

with a monster on a mission
hungry for waste.
You need me. So feed me.

Mind the Gap

Platforms are dangerous
The line is alive
Fall, and a ghost train
May shortly arrive.

25

Hide and Seek

When I played as a kid
How I longed to be caught,

But whenever I hid
Nobody sought.

Friends

Everyone's a friend of someone
Although it seems to me
That every friend has got a friend
Who's not a friend of me.

But there's someone out there looking
For a friend like me, I'm sure
And when we find each other
We'll be friends for evermore.

The Friendship

I was lonely on the island
When I saw a distant mast,
I rushed down to the seashore
But the friendship sailed right past.

Stop, Thief!

There's something about the seaside
I don't understand.

Who steals the footprints
We leave in the sand?

Posters on the platform

Calling all **7** year olds ...

Celebrate!

It's time to party!

Saturday at 7:00p.m.

Missing

Have you seen these tonsils?

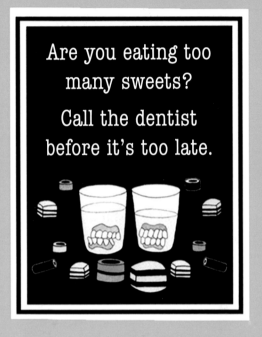

Learning objectives: explore how different texts appeal to readers; choose and prepare poems for performance identifying appropriate expression, tone, volume and use of other voices and sounds; use layout format, graphics and illustrations for different purposes; write non narrative texts using structures of different text types

Curriculum links: Citizenship: Choices

Interest words: aunt-eater, beguiled, cock the snook, foraging, tittle-tat, tonsillitis, unsurpassed

Resources: ICT

Getting started

This book can be read over two or more guided reading sessions.

- Ask children if they've read other poems by Roger McGough and if they like them. Discuss any favourite poets or poems the children have read, and why they like them.

- Ask one of the children to read the blurb to the others and discuss as a group the characters on the cover. What sort of poems do they think will be in this book? Will they be funny or serious?

- Demonstrate how to use the contents on p2, and encourage children to choose some poems they would like to read.

Reading and responding

- Demonstrate reading a poem and encourage children to offer feedback on both your performance and the poem.

- Ask children in pairs to practise reading to each other the poems they have chosen from the contents.

- Remind children to have a go at reading tricky words, and make a note of them to discuss with the group later.